Richmond upon Thames Libraries

Renew online at www.richmond.gov.uk/libraries

LONDON BOROUGH OF
RICHMOND UPON THAMES

For Arlo & Zachary - SL

For Caroline & Cosmo - ES

SIMON & SCHUSTER
First published in Great Britain in 2019 by Simon & Schuster UK Ltd, 1st Floor, 222 Gray's Inn Road, London WC1X 8HB • A CBS Company • Text copyright © 2019 Susannah Lloyd • Illustrations copyright © 2019 Ellie Snowdon The right of Susannah Lloyd and Ellie Snowdon to be identified as the author and illustrator of this work has been asserted by them in accordance with the Copyright, Designs and Patents Act, 1988 • All rights reserved, including the right of reproduction in whole or in part in any form • A CIP catalogue record for this book is available from the British Library upon request • ISBN: 978-1-4711-6560-3 (HB) • ISBN: 978-1 4711-6561-0 (PB) ISBN: 978-1-4711-6562-7 (eBook) • Printed in China • 10 9 8 7 6 5 4 3 2 1

FOX AT LARGE! DAILY SQUEAL

WANTED

TRICKSTER WILEY FOX

DISPLAY DO NOT TAKE

Petunia's Pretty Blooms

THE TERRIBLY FRIENDLY FOX

SUSANNAH LLOYD AND ELLIE SNOWDON

SIMON & SCHUSTER

London New York Sydney Toronto New Delhi

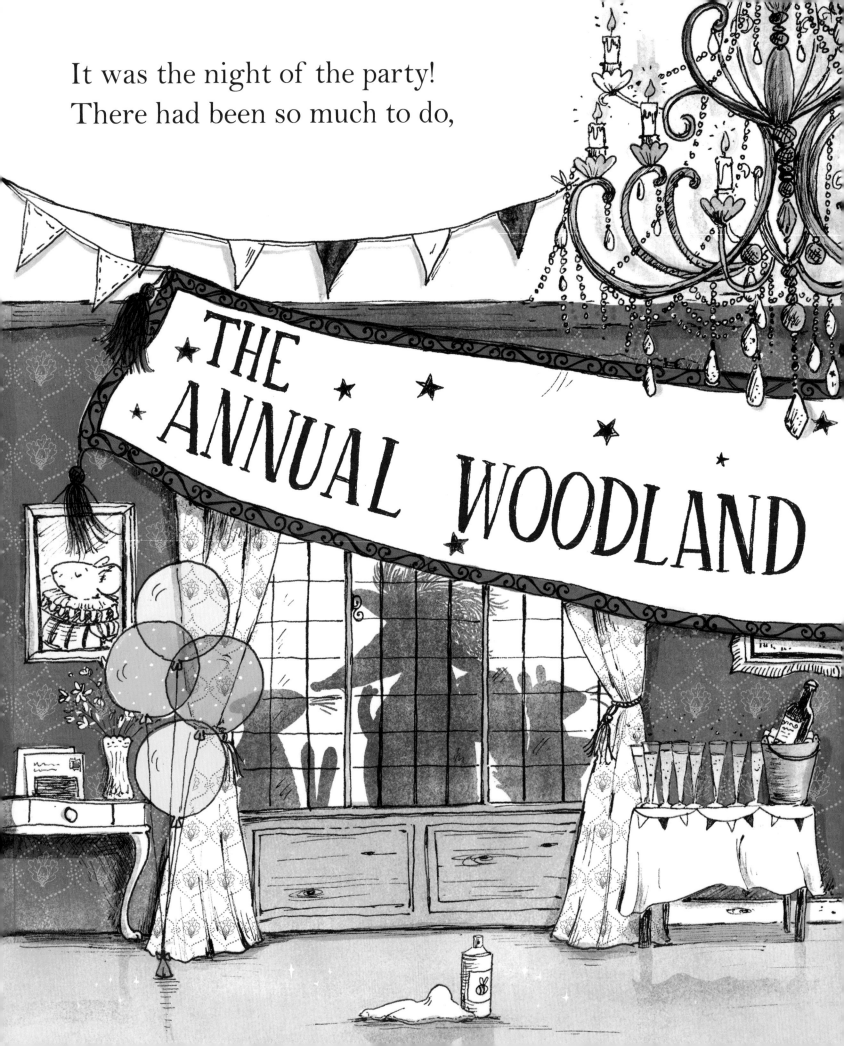

It was the night of the party!
There had been so much to do,

but now the dance floor was polished
and the chandelier was shining.

And this was the finishing touch. "Ta Da!"

CREATURES' BALL!

Just in time too, because here were the guests.

How splendid they looked!

I was wearing my new bow tie.
Quite daring, though I do say so myself.

But then a quite unexpected guest arrived . . .

Oh dear me!
Several of the elderly rabbits fainted,
and Mr Wilberforce hid in the trifle.
After all, we had heard some rather alarming
things about foxes.

And this *was*
The Wiley Fox,
was it not?

But it turned out we had misunderstood.
He explained that he was an entirely reformed
character. He had changed his name to Gerald,
and was now a vegetarian.

Well . . .

We needn't have worried.

Gerald turned out to be the life and soul of the party!

CREATURES' BALL!

YOU'RE NEXT

He proposed a toast, "To new friends!"

How very charming. Such delightful manners, too.

But it looked like some of our guests were a little late for dinner. I *do* hope Gerald didn't think they were being rude.

And boy, that fox could sing!

But, goodness me, who had forgotten to eat up their delicious puddings? And why ever did the music end so suddenly?

Anyway, no one seemed to mind,
because Gerald was making the most
marvellous balloons for everyone.

Even the voles, who are
usually so shy and retiring,
were queuing up to get one.

"Don't let go, now!"

And then, Gerald had the most amusing idea!
What could be better than a spot of musical chairs?

"Ready, steady, go!" I squeaked.

Only . . . how very odd. Someone must have put out too many chairs.

No matter, because after that, Gerald put on
a dazzling show of conjuring tricks.

He even made Lady Agatha's
gold pocket watch disappear
before our very eyes!

"Bravo!" we all cried.

Gerald promised he would make a few
more things disappear later on,
if we insisted.

Do you know, I don't think we had ever met anyone quite so suave and debonair!

Why, he even swept Margaret clean off her feet!

How we all lost ourselves in the dancing.

Talk about the time of our lives!

Whatever was next?

Oh yes! As Gerald said, a party isn't a party without a game of hide-and-seek.

"No peeking!" I promised.

"5, 4, 3, 2, 1...
Coming, ready or not!"

Wherever were they all?

What clever hiding places
they must have found.

But how very rude I was . . . I almost forgot to offer Gerald one of our little nibbles.
He said not to worry, the other guests had been keeping him well-fed. In fact, he was a trifle full, but might be able to fit in just

one

last

bite.

Now the night was nearly over.
There was just enough time to play
Pin the Tail on the Donkey.

Mind you, it did turn out
to be a tad more tricky
than I thought, what with
the polished floor . . .

ATURES' BALL !

"Whoopsie!

Terribly sorry, Madam!
Do please excuse me."

You know, I'm surprised we didn't
have some sort of an accident!

"Well I never!" I gasped.
It turned out I'd hit the target after all!

But my goodness me! Where was everyone?
I suppose they must have all gone home.

Well, I'm sure I speak for us all
when I say it was the best party
we've ever had!

But I *was* rather exhausted.
Perhaps Gerald can host the party next year?